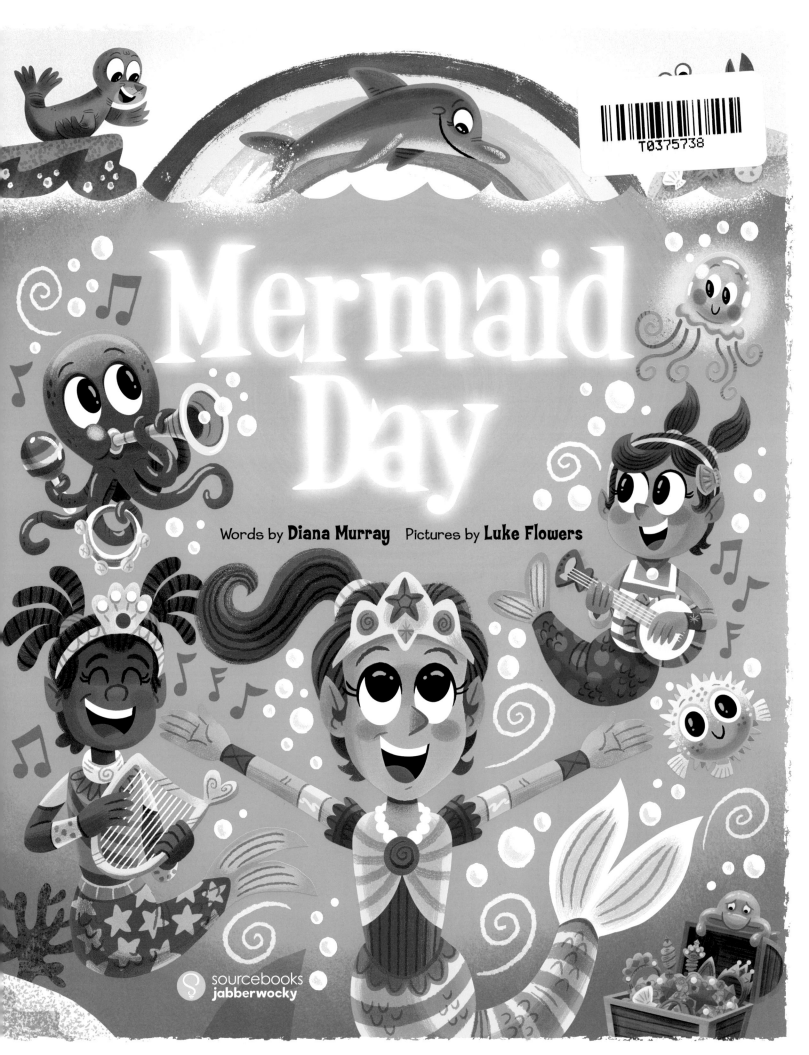

Mermaid Day

Words by **Diana Murray**   Pictures by **Luke Flowers**

sourcebooks
jabberwocky

For my mer-girls, Kate and Jane.
—DM

For Rhonda Jenkins. A whale-sized THANK YOU for the ocean of inspiration, encouragement, and joy you are to me and all your little book buddies. Your creativity and love of books will always make your library a place to discover a lifelong love of reading!
—LF

Text © 2023 by Diana Murray • Illustrations © 2023 by Luke Flowers • Cover and internal design © 2023 by Sourcebooks • Sourcebooks and the colophon are registered trademarks of Sourcebooks. • All rights reserved. • The characters and events portrayed in this book are fictitious or are used fictitiously. Any similarity to real persons, living or dead, is purely coincidental and not intended by the author. • The full colour art was sketched and painted in Photoshop using a wide range of unique digital brushes. • Published by Sourcebooks Jabberwocky, an imprint of Sourcebooks Kids • P.O. Box 4410, Naperville, Illinois 60567-4410 • (630) 961-3900 • sourcebookskids.com • Source of Production: Wing King Tong Paper Products Co. Ltd., Shenzhen, Guangdong Province, China • Date of Production: January 2023 • Run Number: 5029081 • Printed and bound in China. • WKT 10 9 8 7 6 5 4 3 2 1

Mermaid Party

Hooray! Hooray!
It's Mermaid Day!
Beneath the waves that splish and splash,
the mer-queen throws a great big bash!

She decorates with seaweed bows
and seashell garlands hung in rows.
And thanks to sea snails on the scene,
the castle's never looked so clean!

CREAK! The tall gate opens wide,
and all her mer-friends swim inside.

The mer-queen welcomes every guest
and leads them to her treasure chest.
Some necklaces? Or sparkly rings?
(Mermaids love bright, shiny things!)

Dressed up in their favourite bling,
the mermaids strum their harps and sing.

Hooray! Hooray! It's Mermaid Day!
Shake your tail fins! Splash and play!

The grey whales hum as turtles drum.
Their song rings out…and *more* guests come!

The anglerfish and jellies glow
as fairy fish put on a show,
and trumpetfish play happy tunes,
while pufferfish float like balloons!

Creatures of all kinds appear!
The streamers fly! The mermaids cheer!

They dance with dolphins—twirl and glide—
then take a magic seahorse ride!

And tossing rings is so much fun
when narwhals try to catch each one!

But who's that peeking from the dark?
Is that a sh-sh-sh-sh...

RK!?

Panicked fish swim left and right...

YIKES!!

...but mermaids know this shark won't bite.
He's just too shy to come and dance.
They hold his fin. Now here's his chance!

He boogie-woogies, spins, and grooves.
That shark's got some fin-tastic moves!

The mermaids strum and sing their song,
as dolphins *click-clack-squeak* along.

Hooray! Hooray!
It's Mermaid Day!
Shake your tail fins!
Splash and play!

Diving mermaids,
Swish, Swish, Swish,
Catch a sea star,
make a wish.

Bubbles popping,
one, two, three.
mermaid magic
fills the sea!

After singing, loud and proud,
it's time to feed the hungry crowd.

It wouldn't feel like Mermaid Day
without a mer-velous buffet!
The seaweed tea is warm and sweet
and plankton cakes are such a treat.

The moonlight shines. The tide is high.
The mermaids yawn and wave goodbye.

The sleepy mer-queen thanks each guest.

GOODNIGHT

Her weary tail could use some rest.

The guests swim back to cosy caves
and kelp beds rocked beneath the waves.

The most mer-mazing party ends
with sweet dreams in a sea of friends.

SWEET DREAMS